To Ben & R

BEDTIME, ZACHARY!

BEDTIME, ZACHARY!

Muriel Blaustein

Harper & Row, Publishers

To young kids . . . to old kids.

Bedtime, Zachary!
Copyright © 1987 by Muriel Blaustein
Printed in Singapore. All rights reserved.
1 2 3 4 5 6 7 8 9 10
First Edition

Library of Congress Cataloging-in-Publication Data
Blaustein, Muriel.
    Bedtime, Zachary!
    Summary: Mr. and Mrs. Tiger have a hard time
convincing their energetic cub, Zachary, to go to bed
at night until they change roles and let him pretend
to be the parent.
    [1. Tigers—Fiction. 2. Bedtime—Fiction.
3. Parent and child—Fiction] I. Title.
PZ7.B61625Be 1987   [E]   86-45772
ISBN 0-694-00191-0
ISBN 0-06-020537-7 (lib. bdg.)

After supper was Zachary's bedtime.

Zachary was good at making noise, at chasing mice,

at creeping up and pulling his Mom's tail…

and at hiding.

He just wasn't sleepy.

Zachary had an idea.

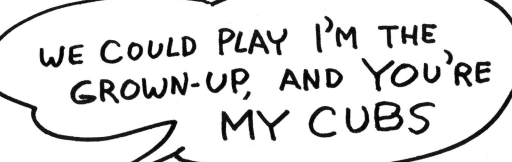

He thought, "I'll be a good parent,
and let them stay up late."

Mr. and Mrs. Tiger agreed.

Zachary changed into grown-up clothes,

and Mr. and Mrs. Tiger changed into their pajamas.

First Zachary let them watch TV.

But Mr. and Mrs. Tiger were good.

Zachary had another idea.

Then Zachary went into the kitchen.

But they didn't want ice-cream sundaes, either.

Zachary wondered what to do.

Mr. and Mrs. Tiger
thought the same thing.

So Zachary was BAD.

And Mr. and Mrs. Tiger were BAD, too.

First they hid.

Then they made noise.

Mr. Tiger chased mice,

and Mrs. Tiger pulled Zachary's tail.

After a while Mr. and Mrs. Tiger did so much playing...

and Zachary did so much chasing...

that they all got to be VERY good at sleeping.